Joe's Car

First published 2001 by
A & C Black (Publishers) Ltd
37 Soho Square
London WID 3QZ

Text copyright © Citizenship Foundation 2001
Illustrations copyright © Tim Archbold 2001

ISBN 0-7136-5846-0

A CIP catalogue for this book is available from
the British Library.

Published in conjunction with the
Citizenship Foundation.
Sponsored by British Telecom.

Printed in Malta on behalf of
Midas printing (UK) Ltd.

Joe's Car

by Annabelle Dixon

Illustrated by Tim Archbold

A & C Black • London

Ben, Joe and Charlie were in the
same class at school.

Sometimes they played together...

...and sometimes they didn't.

One day Ben found a shiny red car under
the old tree in the playground.

He took it in with him at the end of playtime.

"Let me see that car, Ben," said Miss Brunton.
"Where did you get it?"
"I found it," said Ben.

"Joe has lost a car like that,"
said Miss Brunton.
"He says that Charlie ran off
with it and hid it somewhere."

"No one was hiding it when I found it,"
said Ben.
"It's mine now. Joe's car is
probably down a drain."

Just then Joe and Charlie
walked up.

"Hey, that's my car," Joe said.
"That's the one Charlie ran away with and hid."

"No. Your car's down a drain," said Ben.
"This is my car. I found it."

"I think this is Joe's car," said Miss Brunton
to the three boys at once.

She turned and looked at Charlie.
"Why did you hide it, Charlie?" she asked.

"Well, Joe wouldn't let me have a turn with it,"
Charlie said.

"Why didn't you play with something else?"
Miss Brunton asked.

Charlie shook his head.
"All the playground things are broken," he said.

"Where did you hide it, Charlie?"
Miss Brunton asked.

"By the old tree, Miss," said Charlie,
looking at the floor.

Miss Brunton looked at Ben, who was still holding
the car tightly, but she didn't say anything.

Slowly, very slowly, Ben gave the car back to Joe.

"Now will you play together nicely?"
asked Miss Brunton.

But Joe did something Miss Brunton
did not expect him to do.
He put the car away in his back-pack.

"I'm not playing cars any more," he said.
"Charlie will only run off with it again."

"I won't if you share it," said Charlie.

"OK then," Joe said, "but you must
promise not to run off with it."

"All right, I promise," said Charlie.

And they walked off.
They were friends again.

"Can I play too?" asked Ben.
"Actually, I really like red cars like that."

Charlie and Joe looked at each other
and then at Ben.
"Perhaps," they said.

Something to think about...

Parents or teachers can use these questions as starting points for talking to children about the issues raised in the story.

* Joe, Charlie and Ben were friends. What kind of friends were they?

* What do you like about playing together with your friends?

* Do friends ever quarrel? Why? When? What do you do when that happens?

* What do you think about what Charlie did when he hid Joe's car? Why do you think he did that?

* Why do you think Ben kept Joe's car? Was it all right to do that?

* What does 'finders keepers' mean? Is it ever all right to keep things that you find?

* What does it mean when something belongs to you? What should other people do if they want to use it or play with it? Why is that?

* Joe hadn't let Charlie have a turn with his car. Was that all right, do you think? When is taking turns a good thing?

* Why were the playground things broken? What do you think should be done about that?

* What happens when we all share things in school? Who do they belong to? How should we look after them? Why?

* Where else do we find things that belong to all of us? Where do they come from? Who pays for them?

* How do you think Joe was feeling without his car? Think of lots of words to describe his feelings.

* How do you think Ben was feeling when he gave the car back to Joe? Why do you think this?

* Should Ben and Charlie get into trouble for what they did? What would you do if you were the teacher?

* What do you think about what Joe did when he got his car back? Do you think it is ever OK not to take turns?

* What do you think happens at the end of the story? Why were Joe and Charlie unsure about playing with Ben? Was that fair or not?

* Who do you feel most sorry for at the end of the story?

* Think about times when this kind of thing has happened to you. What did you do and how did you feel?

* Are there some good rules which would help us in situations like this?